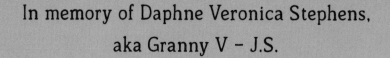

In memory of Daphne Veronica Stephens,
aka Granny V – J.S.

For Grandma,
a piece of me always – B.S.

BLOOMSBURY CHILDREN'S BOOKS
Bloomsbury Publishing Plc
50 Bedford Square, London, WC1B 3DP, UK
29 Earlsfort Terrace, Dublin 2, Ireland

BLOOMSBURY, BLOOMSBURY CHILDREN'S BOOKS and the Diana logo are trademarks of Bloomsbury Publishing Plc

First published in Great Britain in 2022 by Bloomsbury Publishing Plc
This paperback edition published in 2023 by Bloomsbury Publishing Plc

A catalogue record for this book is available from the British Library

ISBN PB: 978 1 5266 1804 7
ISBN eBook: 978 1 5266 1805 4

2 4 6 8 10 9 7 5 3 1

Printed and bound in China by Leo Paper Products, Heshan, Guangdong

FSC
www.fsc.org

MIX
Paper from
responsible sources
FSC® C020056

To find out more about our authors and books visit www.bloomsbury.com and sign up for our newsletters

The
MISSING
Piece

Written by
**Jordan
STEPHENS**

Illustrated by
**Beth
SUZANNA**

BLOOMSBURY
CHILDREN'S BOOKS
LONDON   OXFORD   NEW YORK   NEW DELHI   SYDNEY

The only thing that Sunny loved more than chocolate biscuits
was the sweet, dusty chaos of an unfinished jigsaw puzzle.

Sunny adored the way the pieces
hugged one another.

Every piece was connected
and every piece was important.
And the more loving the pieces were,
the more worldly, wicked and wonderful
the picture became.

Whenever she finished a puzzle, Sunny would feel a warm, honey-trickle of happiness in her chest.

She wished that she could hold on to that feeling forever – wrap it around her body or pour it into a bottle.

But the feeling **always** disappeared.
The only way she could keep it coming
was by completing puzzle . . .

after puzzle . . .

after puzzle.

"What if I complete **every** jigsaw puzzle, Gran?
Will I be sad forever?"

"Listen, Sunshine," said Gran.
  "Do you **really** believe that finishing
puzzles is what makes you happy?"

"Yes!" said Sunny, gazing up at her tree of a grandmother.
She was definitely Sunny's favourite tree.
She even smelled like bark
and was **wonderful** to hug.

Gran smiled and took Sunny's hand.
"Well then, you'll **want** to see this . . ."

Sunny followed Gran indoors, where the floors
smelled like old flowers and the walls
like apple stew with cinnamon.

"Let's see if you can finish this one!"
she said, handing Sunny
a faded, tattered box.

Sunny had encountered a universe of mystery,
but NEVER a jigsaw puzzle with this many pieces.

She started right away.

Time zoomed by and soon Sunny was seconds away
from that buzz. Moments from being a honeybee.
She reached into the giant jigsaw box for the final time,
only to find that one piece was . . .

Sunny's tummy flipped
like a fish out of water.
"I HAVE to finish it, Gran.
Who did the puzzle last?"

"Let me think," replied Gran. "I lent it
to the Jack family next door. Their dad,
Ken, fixes watches and makes jam."

"Can I go and ask?" said Sunny.

"Yes. I'll be right here," Gran said.

Sunny felt very grown-up as she walked down the path. She gazed at the rows of houses which hugged the curve of the road.

They looked like little teeth on a street that was smiling.

The Jack family's house smelled of warm bread
and looked like milky tea.

Sunny knocked on the door and Violet,
the youngest of the Jack family, answered.

"Hello, I'm Sunny and I'm looking for the **missing piece**
from Gran's really big jigsaw puzzle.
It's **very** important.
Have you seen it?"

"Sorry, no," said Violet. "We finished it
and passed it on to the Patel family next door.
Come on, I'll **help** you find it!"

As they skipped down the path together,
Sunny and Violet said more words
to each other than their
steps combined.

They discovered that they **both**
loved climbing, finding insects
and mixing all the parts
of their dinner together.

The Patel house smelled of spices and
looked like a waving candle.

A boy called Ravi answered the door.

"Hello, I'm Sunny and I'm looking for the missing piece from Gran's really big jigsaw puzzle. It's **very** important. Have you seen it?"

Ravi shook his head. Sunny's heart sank.

"But," he said, "after we finished the puzzle we lent it to the Stephens family down the road. Maybe it's there? I'd like to help."

Sunny and Violet raced off down the street.

"Hey wait!" Ravi called after them. "Come and see these first!"

Moments later they were all peering over a
garden wall at a patch of sunflowers.

"Did you know that no matter where you plant these,"
said Ravi, "they will always grow to face the sun?"

"Hey, maybe they'll face you,
Sunny!" said Violet.

The Stephens house smelled like an ocean breeze
and looked like a coral reef.

Ravi rang the doorbell. Sunny crossed her fingers and Violet
held her breath. A young boy answered the door.
"Hello! I'm Gabriel. How can I help you?"

"Hello, I'm Sunny. We're looking for the missing piece
to Gran's really big jigsaw puzzle!
It's very important!"

Gabriel agreed that it was really important but, unfortunately,
he had no idea where the missing piece was.

"I'll help you look for it tomorrow," he said. "But it's getting
late and we should get you back to your gran's."

And so, as the light was running from the day,
they made their way back, stepping on each other's
shadows and making plans for the future.

Sunny's gran opened the door to find
the whole gang smiling.

"Did you find the missing piece?" she asked.

Sunny shook her head. "No, but I don't mind
because I made loads of new friends
and we danced with the SKY."

Gran smiled, reached into her pocket and pulled out . . .

. . . the missing piece!

"Do you still think that it's only finishing puzzles that makes you happy, Sunny?"

Sunny was speechless and felt warm.
She'd always known that her gran
was really smart.

"Of all the puzzles you've
ever given me, Gran," said Sunny,
"that's definitely my favourite one."